A Very Braden Christmas

A Braden Short Story

Love in Bloom Series

Melissa Foster

ISBN-13: 978-1-948868-33-4
ISBN-10: 1-948868-33-4

A VERY BRADEN CHRISTMAS

Cover Design: Elizabeth Mackey Designs

WORLD LITERARY PRESS
PRINTED IN THE UNITED STATES OF AMERICA

For my fans, for loving my Bradens
as much as I do.

Dear Readers,

I have wanted to write a holiday story for the Bradens of Weston for years, and I am thrilled to have finally fit it into my writing schedule. Hal Braden's love, loyalties, and strong family values are the foundations upon which I've built the stories found in the Love in Bloom series. I look forward to providing more peeks into his relationship with his late wife, Adriana, and I hope this novelette fills you with happiness the way it has for me.

If this is your first Love in Bloom story, "A Very Braden Christmas" is a great way to get to know the family. Then you can go back and read each couple's love story. All characters from the Love in Bloom big-family romance collection appear in other family series. (For example, the Bradens at Weston also appear in The Remingtons, The Ryders, and Seaside Summers, as well as all of the other Love in Bloom subseries.)

All Love in Bloom books can be read as stand-alone novels, in any order, but for the most enjoyment you might want to read them in publication order. A checklist is available for download on the Reader Goodies page on my website: www.MelissaFoster.com/RG

Sign up for my newsletter to receive a free Braden/Remington short story and to be notified of new releases and events: www.MelissaFoster.com/News

Happy reading!
Melissa

Chapter One

THE STAR IS CROOKED.

Hal Braden smiled as the voice of his beloved wife, Adriana, whispered through his mind, as real as the bitter winter chill stinging his cheeks. He gazed up at the star on the peak of the barn roof, glittering against the backdrop of the Colorado mountains, and sure enough, the star was crooked. He shook his head, laughing softly, and swore he could hear Adriana's playful giggle as he remembered how they used to duck into the barn office, or one of the horse stalls, for a little *afternoon delight* when their six children were playing outside. After one such secret steamy moment, Adriana had noticed the star was crooked and she'd told Hal it was because their love was too big to be confined and they'd rocked the entire world.

"Oh, darlin'," he said in the soft, gravelly voice that seemed to come only when he spoke to her, "if only that were the case today."

He heard Adriana's voice often, only sometimes his beloved wife didn't *whisper* from the grave; she outright hammered him for messing up one thing or another. After all these years, that was okay with Hal. Not a day went by that he didn't wish he could pull her into his arms and tell her one last time how much he adored her, that his every breath carried as much hurt as love and that he looked forward to the day he'd be with her again.

He pulled his Stetson down low against the cold evening air as he headed toward the barn, leading Hope, the old chestnut mare he'd bought for Adriana when they'd first found out she was ill so many years ago. Hope had far outlived Hal's wife, whom they'd lost to cancer when their youngest, Hugh, was just a toddler. Hope had slowed down over the years, but Hal swore Adriana's spirit lived on in the horse, who refused to give in to the inevitable.

Hope stopped walking and bobbed her head in the direction of Hal's stone and cedar house, just up the hill from the barn. His son Josh's Land Rover was pulling into the driveway. Josh and his wife, Riley, were world-renowned fashion designers. They had a little girl named Abigail, who was just shy of two years old, and they split their time between Manhattan and Weston, Colorado.

Hal gazed at Hope and petted her jaw as he said,

"They're all moving home, darlin', just like we always wanted."

About the same time that Josh and Riley had decided to move back to Weston part time, Hugh and his wife, Brianna, had moved back full time. They'd purchased a home with a guesthouse for Brianna's mother just a few miles away from Hal. Treat, Hal's eldest, who owned resorts all over the world, and Rex, who ran the family ranch, both lived within walking distance with their families. Savannah, Hal's only daughter, had a cabin in the mountains not far from Hal's. Only Dane had yet to move back. As the founder of the Brave Foundation, Dane dedicated his life to saving sharks, and he lived on a boat with his wife, Lacy, and their little boy, Finn.

"Let's get you inside, Hope, so we don't miss the festivities."

Every Christmas Eve since his children were born, Hal and his family attended the community barn dance, after which they had a slumber party in Hal's living room. It had been Adriana's idea to start the tradition. *Just a little something special so they always remember how important family is.* Getting the kids into the living room for a slumber party with their old man when they were teenagers had been dicey, with plenty of huffs and rolled eyes. But in the end it had taken only one of the children reminding the others that they were carrying on the tradition for their mother for them all to comply. And now that all of Hal's children had families of their own, Christmas Eve was even more chaotic—and more meaningful. Rex and Treat had taken the children out to cut down the tree, and everyone had helped decorate it. It had been a loud, exciting day, and the evening promised to be even more so.

Hal pulled open the heavy wooden door to the barn and led Hope inside. As scents of leather, livestock, and family greeted him, years of memories rushed in. He'd been around horses his whole life and was proud to carry on his family's legacy breeding Dutch Warmblood show jumpers. Ranch life was grueling work, toiling in the hot sun and the frigid snow from predawn until well after dark, but he wouldn't trade it for the world.

Hope whinnied, bobbing her big head and pawing at the ground.

"What is it, girl?" Hal cocked his head, listening to the familiar sounds of the barn, and then he heard what Hope must have already taken note of. *Shuffling.* The sound came from the office in the back of the barn. The door was ajar, and Hal wondered what critter had found its way in. He heard a crash as he opened Hope's stall, and she neighed and shook her head, stepping back.

"You stubborn old girl. I don't have time for this today."

Hope pushed her muzzle into his sternum. At six foot six, Hal was still broad and thick-chested, despite his gray hair and beard. Working on the ranch kept him in prime shape, but he was no match for the softness in Hope's eyes.

He kissed her muzzle and said, "What is it, darlin'? I can handle any vermin. You know that."

Hope blew out a breath, a sound Hal knew well. It was Hope's way of saying, *No shit. Just leave it alone anyway.* But Hal had a gathering to attend, and he wasn't about to let an animal tear up his office. Another crash sounded, propelling Hal into action.

"Let's go." He hauled Hope into her stall and strode determinedly toward the office, readying himself for an angry critter.

He snagged a pitchfork that was leaning against the wall by the office and rolled his shoulders back as another heavy *thud* sounded. He ground out a curse as he threw the door open, pitchfork raised—and froze at the sight of his son Rex holding his wife, Jade, against the far wall, her legs wrapped around his waist. The murderous look in Rex's eyes as he glowered over his shoulder was enough to scare off an army of men.

But not Hal Braden.

Hal's deep laughter filled the room as he set down the

pitchfork and said, "No wonder the star was crooked."

"Christ," Rex growled, the muscles in his jaw jumping beneath his pitch-black scruff.

Rex was the most aggressive and ornery of Hal's children. He reminded Hal of himself in his younger years. With bulbous biceps and tree-trunk legs, born from years of hard manual labor, Rex would not shy away from any battle—including one with his father. He'd gone against Hal's wishes when he'd fallen for Jade Johnson, the daughter of Hal's arch nemesis. But it was Rex's love for Jade that had mended a forty-plus-year feud between the two families, reuniting Hal and his one-time best friend.

Rex's brows slanted. "Ya mind, Pop?"

"The woman just had a baby a few weeks ago. Give her a break." He snickered and backed toward the door.

Rex scoffed, a smile tugging at his lips. "*She* attacked *me*."

Jade's cheeks burned red despite her being fully dressed. She buried her face in Rex's neck, mumbling an apology.

"Now, get outta here so I can make out with my wife in private," Rex said with a smile. "Lord knows we never get a moment alone anymore." Hal's oldest son, Treat, and the others were watching Rex and Jade's toddler, Little Hal, and their new baby girl, Josslyn Adriana.

"A'right. Josh's family is here, so I imagine we're head-

ing out soon." He turned to leave and said, "You're fixin'
the damn star."

Rex growled his agreement, and Hal walked out with a
smile on his face.

AFTER TAKING CARE of Hope and the other horses,
Hal headed up to the house. His sons Dane and Hugh met
him on the patio. All of Hal's boys shared his tall, broad
stature, dark hair, and dark eyes, but Hugh's eyes were a
shade lighter than the others, and at the moment they
sparked with mischief.

"The kids are getting antsy," Dane said. "Savannah and
Jack arrived while you were in the barn. I think we ought
to get going before the boys find their way into too much
trouble."

"If we can find Rex and Jade. And *yes*, we checked the
bedrooms," Hugh said with a coy smile. Adriana had
known the minute their youngest was born that Hugh
would be a rascally one, and she'd been right. Hugh was a
race-car driver, and until he'd met Brianna, he'd enjoyed
all the fruits of his success and celebrity. Now the father of
two, with another due in February, Hugh was an excellent
father and a loving husband. He made Hal proud, as all his

children did.

Hal grinned. "They're down in the barn. Give 'em a few minutes."

Dane nudged Hugh and raised his brows.

"Aw, hell no. That's not happening. Let's go, bro," Hugh said. "If I can't drag my wife up to a bedroom, he's not touching his."

As they jogged toward the barn Hal shook his head, chuckling at his boys' antics. He hoped they'd carry on that playful, brotherly banter forever.

"Hi, Daddy!" Savannah ran out the back door, looking so much like a young Adriana, Hal's heart thudded a little harder as she threw her arms around him. Savannah was an entertainment attorney, working three days a week in Manhattan now that she and her husband, Jack Remington, had a son, Adam, who was three. Savannah was as feisty and stubborn as her mother had been, which was a good thing, considering she was a middle child who had grown up surrounded by boisterous, overprotective brothers.

"Hello, sweetheart. How's my girl? Did you have a nice visit with Jack's family?"

"Yes. They're all doing well. His parents are overjoyed with all their grandbabies. Dex and Ellie's new baby boy, Lucas, reminds me of Treat and Jack," she said as they went inside. "You know, *serious, watchful*. He's only a baby, but I can see it."

Hal chuckled, enjoying the bustle and noise of his grandchildren and daughters-in-law. Lacy and Brianna were in the kitchen decorating cookies, while Hugh's boy, Christian, and Treat's son, Dylan, darted in and out, trying to sneak a few off the counter.

"Christian Braden!" Brianna said with a smile as her little boy snagged a cookie and tore from the room in a fit of giggles. She ran a hand over her seven-month baby bump and shook her head.

Christian and Dylan were a handful, racing around with superhero capes, climbing on the couch as Treat's wife, Max, who was cradling baby Josslyn in a rocking chair, reminded them not to stand on Grandpa's furniture. Little Hal and Adam were racing toy cars in the hallway, cheering loudly, and amid all the chaos, Hugh's daughter, Layla, who had grown into a thoughtful and beautiful young teenager, and Treat's daughter, Adriana, who was the spitting image of her late grandmother, sat huddled together, talking in whispers in Hal's favorite recliner. Treat sat in an armchair, reading to his youngest boy, one-year-old Bryce, while keeping a watchful eye on everyone.

"Grandpa Hal! Play with us!" Dylan hollered as he ran by, chasing Finn, who was carrying a Christmas gift he'd taken from under the tree.

Finn darted behind Hal, all blond curls like Lacy and big dark eyes like Dane, and cried, "Papa Hal! Help!"

Hal picked up a squealing Dylan, holding him above his head as Finn laughed hysterically, clinging to the present.

Finn jumped up and down, trying to reach his cousin. "Let him down, Papa Hal! I want to play chase!"

"What do you say I wrap you up and put *you* under the tree?" Hal said to Dylan, trying to temper his smile.

"Yes! Do it!" Dylan said, causing Hal and Treat to laugh heartily.

"Do it! Do it!" Christian chanted, and as if it were a call of the wild beckoning a herd, the other two younger boys barreled into the room.

Adam, Finn, and Little Hal all jumped up and down around Grandpa Hal's feet as he held Dylan hostage. The little boys chanted, "Do it! Do it! Do it!"

Rex, Jade, Dane, and Hugh came in from outdoors. Rex took one look at the mayhem, picked up Little Hal, and turned him upside down, holding him by his ankles as his boy giggled and wiggled. "Caught myself a rabbit!"

Dane followed suit with Finn and exclaimed, "Got mine!"

As Hugh reached for Christian, his boy took off in a fit

of giggles across the living room. Hugh took chase, and as he snagged his boy around the waist, earning a squeal of glee, Hal's gaze fell to the picture of Adriana smiling down on him from the mantel, and his heart felt fuller than it ever had.

Chapter Two

PRACTICALLY THE WHOLE town turned out for the annual Christmas barn dance. Colorful lights were strewn over the dance floor, and a massive Christmas tree anchored one side of the makeshift stage, where the band was playing. Children, dressed in their holiday best, ran around with cookies and punch while their parents danced and mingled. Hugh had never thought he'd move back to Weston, a small ranch town where gossip traveled faster than the speed of light and the main drag was built to replicate the Wild West. It had all seemed hokey when he was younger, and he couldn't wait to get out in the world and make his mark. Now, surrounded by his siblings and their families as his mother-in-law danced with his father and he danced with his beautiful wife, while watching Christian run around with his cousins and Layla whisper with her school friends, he couldn't imagine living anywhere else.

"Hey, baby." Hugh nuzzled against Brianna's neck and said, "Want to sneak out to the car?"

Her soft brown eyes simmered with heat. She was the sexiest woman, the sweetest mother, and the best friend Hugh had ever known. He counted himself lucky for the blind-date-gone-wrong that had ended with his meeting Brianna.

"You know I would, but with this belly, we'd need to find a motor home," she said, rubbing her burgeoning baby bump. Her eyes turned serious, shifting to Layla talking with a boy beneath the mistletoe, and she said, "But we can't. That's Easton, the boy Layla likes, and she might get her first kiss tonight."

Hugh's chest tightened. "*What?* She's barely a teenager."

"And she has a crush, Hugh," Brianna said with a smile.

Hugh watched their daughter smiling and blushing at the lanky blond boy before her, and all he could think about was the innocent almost-six-year-old little girl full of hopes and dreams of finding her Prince Charming she'd been when he'd first met her. She'd called him *Prince Hugh*, and he'd melted inside. Now she was under the mistletoe with some boy looking to steal her first kiss? A kiss she could never get back? A kiss that would surely start her on the path of wanting *more* kisses? Hugh gritted his teeth. *No fucking way.*

"Daddy's britches in a twist over his little girl?" Max teased as she and Treat danced beside them. "Oh no, brace yourself for the cavalry." She motioned toward Josh, Rex, and Dane, heading their way with determined looks on their faces.

"You see what's going on over there?" Josh sidled up to them with Abigail in his arms and said, "Abi isn't dating until she's *thirty.*"

"Right?" Hugh huffed. "They're standing *way* too close beneath the mistletoe." He stepped back from Brianna, but she held tightly to his arms. Her long dark hair framed her gorgeous face, and Layla looked just like her. Hugh had always known Layla would attract boys, but he hadn't expected it to be so soon. He wasn't ready for this.

"Hugh, *relax,*" Brianna urged.

"Fuck that," Rex said. He looked like he was going to blow smoke out of his ears, which was exactly how Hugh felt. "We need to intervene."

"I'm in," Dane said.

Treat narrowed his eyes and said, "Agreed. Let's go."

As Josh tried to hand Abigail to Brianna, she said, "No! You cannot do this. You'll *mortify* her."

"I don't give a damn," Hugh said, stepping around her and watching their little girl. "She's our daughter, and that boy is not stealing her first kiss. She'll build fantasies from that kiss, dream of him falling in love with her. And for what? So he can move on to the *next* little girl? Over my dead body."

Brianna put her hands on his cheeks, directing his eyes to hers as she said, "That's what little girls and little boys do. If you screw this up for her, she'll hate you for it."

Hugh's jaw clenched tight. He'd already hit a few rough patches with their emotional tween daughter, when he'd nixed her attending a boy-girl birthday party and again when he'd caught her talking on the phone with a boy. He looked at his brothers, each of whom were also grinding their teeth and shrugging, as if they didn't know if it was true, or maybe as if it didn't matter if it was.

Treat turned to his wife and said, "Max? What do you think?"

"It's true," Max said. "She'll think you're all big pains in her butt and will probably go weeks without talking to any of you. Right now all she's thinking about is how much she hopes that boy will kiss her. She's probably discussed it at length with her girlfriends and even practiced with her pillow."

"I do not need to know about the pillow," Hugh said as

he looked at Layla in her sparkly dress and matching ballet flats. Brianna, Savannah, and his sisters-in-law had spent forever primping and curling Layla's hair for her, and now he understood why. They were all in on it, and Hugh and his brothers hadn't been clued in. When did Layla get so grown up? He'd seen the changes happening over the last two years, as she'd cleaned out her closet, ridding it of fluffy dresses and tiaras, but he hadn't pictured those things being replaced with a boy. And when had his wife started keeping secrets?

"You knew about this first-kiss plan and didn't tell me?" he asked Brianna.

"Oh, please, Hugh," Max said. "Like any of us could tell any of you about a first kiss without you losing your minds?"

"Jade sure as hell better tell me when it's Joss's turn," Rex seethed.

Brianna laughed. "It's part of growing up, a rite of passage, and I'm telling you, Hugh, she'll be livid."

Hugh's protective urges surged forward, and he said, "She'll get over it."

Hugh headed across the barn with his brothers and Brianna in tow, ready to save his little girl from what he was sure would be weeks of a broken heart. As they neared, he heard the group of boys taunting Easton.

"Easton has a crush!" a scrawny redheaded boy said, as another boy made kissing noises.

"Easton has a *girlfriend*!" another boy teased.

"Why don't you *kiss her*, Easton?" a third boy called out, following it up with more kissing noises.

Hugh was going to tear them apart. His hands fisted at his sides as Easton said something to Layla and then took off running out of the barn, with his posse on his heels.

Layla burst into tears and ran in the opposite direction. Hugh's heart shattered.

"I'm going to kill him," Hugh seethed, turning to go after Easton.

Brianna grabbed his hand and said, "He doesn't need you right now. Our daughter does."

"That kid needs to be taught a lesson," Hugh ground out.

"We've got him *and* his friends." Rex looked at their brothers and said, "Let's go teach those boys to be men." Rex, Dane, and Josh went after the boys.

"Damn it," Treat snapped. "Now we're picking fights with middle schoolers?"

As Treat took off after their brothers, Hugh went in search of Layla and found her just outside the back doors, sitting on a haystack on the patio surrounded by her girlfriends. They were patting her on the shoulder, reassuring her and calling Easton all sorts of bad names. Hugh had a few harsh names of his own to add to their list.

Layla wiped her eyes and looked up at him.

Her girlfriends said, "Hi, Mr. Braden," in unison.

"Hi, girls. Would you mind giving me a minute alone with Layla?"

"Sure thing, Mr. Braden," one of her friends said.

They hugged Layla, each leaving her with a word of encouragement, before they walked away in a huddle. He was glad Layla had such close friends, but as he sat beside her, he wished she didn't need them for this particular situation.

"I know what you're going to say," she said sullenly.

Hugh sighed as he took off his jacket and put it around her shoulders. "You do? What's that?"

"That I'm too young to like a boy." She fidgeted with the sparkles on her dress.

Hugh thought about that and about what Brianna had said. "You know what, princess? You're right. I did want to say that, and I wanted to give that boy a piece of my mind, too, for making you cry. But you're not a little girl anymore. You're turning into a beautiful young lady."

Tears welled in her eyes. "I'm not beautiful."

"Oh, honey, you're so very wrong. That boy picked the most beautiful girl in school to like, and that's *really* scary for a boy his age. Heck, it's scary at any age. He didn't run away because he didn't want to kiss you under the mistletoe. He ran away because he wanted to kiss you so much, it scared him."

She nibbled on her lower lip. "That's stupid."

He smiled and said, "Boys are stupid sometimes." He took her small hand in his and said, "I know this hurts right now, and you probably feel like your heart is crushed."

She nodded, and he felt his own heart crumble into pieces again.

"I'm the *only* one of my friends who hasn't kissed a boy," she said woefully.

"Good," slipped out before he could check it, and she slumped beside him. "I don't mean that the way it sounds, sweetheart. What I mean is good, because it means you're not kissing just *any* boy. You're waiting for the right boy."

"Easton *is* the right boy," she said.

"Maybe so," he said, because who the hell knew…It could happen. His own father had met his mother when she was only fourteen, and their love was as true as it got.

"He's smart, and funny, and he draws really well. And I love talking to him, Daddy. He's not like the other boys. He doesn't say stupid stuff." She paused, and then she looked at him with her big brown eyes and said, "Do you remember your first kiss?"

"I do, and do you want to know what I remember most about it?"

She nodded.

"I remember feeling like a champion, because I got my first kiss before all my friends did. That gave me bragging rights, and you know how much I like to brag." That earned him a smile, and he squeezed her hand. "But I don't even remember the girl's name, and do you want to know what I think about my first kiss now?"

She nodded, and he brushed the tears from her cheeks.

"I wish your mom could have been my first kiss, and part of me pretends she was. When I met your mom, she was almost six years into an eighteen-year plan of not kissing any men until you were off to college. You see, princess, my real first kiss was snuck between classes in the hallway of my middle school. And that girl? She kissed me on a *dare*, and that kiss gave *her* bragging rights. But I had to *earn* my kiss with your mom and prove to her and to myself—and to *you*—that I was worthy of it. *That* first kiss was one I'll *never* forget."

She kicked her legs, fidgeted with her dress, and said, "Thanks, Daddy."

Hugh's heart swelled with love. When he'd married Brianna and adopted Layla, he'd dreamed of these moments, of being *Daddy* and helping her through hard times.

"Don't worry, princess. If Easton's supposed to be your first kiss, he will be." He kissed her temple and said, "But maybe next time you want to kiss a boy, you should do it where I don't have to watch, or you might give your old man a heart attack."

She giggled, and Hugh stood up and reached for her hand. "How about you come inside and dance with me?"

She stood up and handed him his jacket. Then she looked sheepishly at the ground, pushing the toe of her ballet flat into the patio. "Um, Daddy?" She glanced inside the barn, where her friends were huddled together, sneaking glances at them. "Would it be okay if we didn't dance right now, and I joined my friends instead?"

So this was what it felt like to be ditched by his little girl. Damn, it stung. "Sure, princess. Go have fun."

"Thank you. I love you!" She bounced on her toes and threw her arms around him, hugging him tight and soothing the sting her growing up had caused.

Chapter Three

MUSIC FLOATED OUT from the barn as Savannah and her sisters-in-law headed outside to wrangle the kids onto the enormous horse-drawn red wagon for their annual Christmas hayride. Sparkling colorful lights lined the wagon. Hal was holding Bryce, who was fast asleep. Treat and Max's little boy looked even smaller in his grandpa's big arms. Finn and Adam were running around in their puffy blue and red parkas and hats and flopping onto their backs in mounds of snow. Dylan and Christian were having a snowball fight and running from Hugh and Treat, slowing long enough only to peg them with snow. Savannah tried to catch Dylan as he ran by, but he slipped through her fingers.

"Incoming!" Savannah hollered to Treat as Dylan wound up to throw a snowball.

What a sight it was to see six-foot-six Treat dodging the

attack. He swooped Dylan into his arms and threw him over his shoulder like a sack of potatoes.

Dylan's arms and legs flailed. "No!" he shouted between fits of giggles. "Dad!"

Adriana was petting one of the gypsy horses, her favorite breed. Savannah's cousin Luke lived in nearby Trusty, Colorado, and provided the horses for the holiday hayrides every year. With bells on their tack, red bows in their abundant, silky manes and tails, and gorgeous feathering completely covering their hooves, the beautiful horses gave the evening a fairy-tale feel.

"Adriana!" Christian shouted.

Adriana turned, and Christian beaned her with a snowball, then took off running.

"Daddy!" Adriana hollered as she ran after Christian.

Without missing a step, Treat scooped Christian up, tossing him over his other shoulder. Both boys hollered and laughed as Treat carried them over to the wagon.

Little Hal ran past Layla, bumping into her and sending her spinning into Jade's legs.

In one swift motion, Rex grabbed Little Hal by the back of his thick blue coat and lifted him up in the air, his son's legs still running, and said, "Boy, what do you say to your cousin Layla?"

"Sorry!" Little Hal hollered.

"You could have hurt her," Rex said sternly. "What'd I tell you about how you should treat girls?"

"*Da-ad!*" Little Hal complained, arms flailing.

Rex narrowed his eyes and said, "Protect girls because…"

"We should!" Little Hal said.

"And be nice because…" Rex urged.

"We can!" Little Hal said with a proud grin. "Okay, Dad! I will!"

Rex lowered him into his arms and said something Savannah couldn't hear. Little Hal nodded vehemently, his face a younger mirror image of his burly father's. Rex set him on his feet.

Little Hal went to Layla and said, "I'm sorry for bumping into you." He wrapped his arms around her, and Layla smiled.

"That right there," Jade said, eyeing Rex as she dropped a kiss onto baby Josslyn's forehead. "That's the best mama porn *ever.*"

Jade's jet-black hair cascaded out from beneath a red knit hat, falling nearly to her waist. Savannah was surprised that Jade had made it to the event having just had a baby a few weeks ago, but Jade never let anything slow her down.

Riley joined them, carrying Abigail, who even at twenty months looked just like her mama, with straight brown hair and hazel eyes that seemed to always be smiling. "Look." She pointed to Dane and Lacy kissing by the barn. "And check out Treat and Max."

Treat and Max were sitting on a hay bale in the wagon kissing, each one holding on to the back of a boy's coat while Christian and Dylan played at their feet.

"Have you noticed that mayhem follows our families?" Riley said.

"I can't believe we're going to be adding to it." Savannah put her hand on her belly.

Riley and Jade looked at her with wide eyes. Riley said, "You're pregnant?"

"We are!" Savannah said happily.

The girls gave her one-armed hugs, congratulating her.

"I'm so excited!" Riley said.

"How far along are you?" Jade asked, and before Savannah could respond, she yelled, "Savannah and Jack are pregnant!"

Cheers and whoops followed as her family gathered around, except Treat and Max, who knew better than to let the *wild boys* loose. They'd never get them back on the wagon for the hayride. Instead, Treat and Max hollered, "Congratulations!"

"Another grandbaby?" Hal exclaimed. He hugged Savannah and said, "No snowbound cabin births this time, okay, darlin'?"

She and Jack had taken a trip to their cabin in the mountains when Savannah was pregnant with Adam, and their bundle of joy had decided to come early. Jack had delivered Adam during a snowstorm.

"Don't worry, Daddy. We're going to move in with you the month before I'm due, just in case," Savannah teased, as strong arms circled her waist from behind. Her husband's bearded cheek brushed over her skin as he kissed her.

"I thought we were waiting until tomorrow at breakfast to tell everyone." Jack's deep voice sent rivers of heat through her body.

"I couldn't wait." She turned in his arms, and he pressed his magnificent lips to hers.

"I'm glad, because I kind of slipped and told Josh earlier." His dark eyes glimmered with love.

"Then Josh is in big trouble for not telling me!" Riley said, turning an expectant smile to Josh.

After hugs and congratulations, everyone finally got on the wagon. The adults sat on hay bales around the sides of the wagon, and the children gathered in the middle on a floor of hay. They were counting heads when Savannah saw Layla and the boy she and her sisters-in-law had stopped Rex and her other brothers from harassing earlier in the night standing by the other wagon. Savannah tapped Brianna's leg, motioning toward them. Brianna grabbed Hugh's hand, and Hugh followed her gaze to the kids just as the boy pressed his lips to Layla's cheek. Hugh's eyes narrowed, and then Layla smiled, touching her cheek absently as she nodded at something the boy said. The boy went into the barn, and Hugh climbed down from the wagon as Layla approached.

"Oh boy," Savannah said softly, worrying that Hugh might give her grief for the kiss.

Hugh reached a hand out to his daughter, pulling her in for a hug. He leaned down, saying something that Savannah couldn't hear, and then Layla hugged him again.

Hugh lifted her onto the wagon, and she ran to Adriana, sitting at Max's feet, and the girls immediately began whispering. Hugh climbed into the wagon, his loving eyes meeting Brianna's as he took his seat beside her.

As the horses began their wintery trek, Bryce was fast asleep in Max's arms. Dylan sat at Treat's feet beside Adriana, playing with the other kids, and Treat was looking at his family like they were the only people in the loud, crowded wagon. Josslyn lay sleeping in Jade's arms, while Rex and Hugh sat sentinel over the mayhem in the middle of the wagon.

Savannah leaned closer to Jack and said, "Should we

tell them the rest of our news?"

It started snowing, causing more commotion as the kids cheered and tipped their faces up toward the sky, opening their mouths to catch snowflakes on their tongues.

Jack's midnight-blue eyes collided with hers, and even after all these years her heart stumbled at their intense connection. Jack had spent several years in the Special Forces. He now worked as a private pilot and ran a survival training program. He'd lost his first wife in a horrendous car accident and had holed away in his mountain cabin for years, until he'd met Savannah and their connection had been too strong to ignore. She had given up on relation-ships when she'd met Jack, but they'd helped each other heal, and she thanked the heavens above for the man, whom she never wanted to live a day without.

When Jack opened his mouth to speak, Dane said, "What news?"

Jack laughed and said, "Guess it's time to share, angel."

"We have news, too," Lacy said, tucking her corkscrew blond curls behind her ear. "You go first."

Savannah laced her fingers with Jack's and said, "I'm moving my legal practice to Weston."

There was a collective gasp, and then everyone spoke at once, asking questions and congratulating them. It was all Savannah could do to smile and try to keep up.

"That's fantastic," Max said. "Will you still work only three days a week?"

"Yes, three days. That's the plan right now," Savannah explained. "Jack and I want to be closer to everyone. We're going to start looking for a place to live so we can get set up before the baby comes, and we'll keep our cabin in the mountains."

Dylan yelled, "Adam's moving here!" sparking another bout of cheers among the children.

"Can I still come to your cabin?" Adriana asked. She loved spending time in the mountains with them.

"Of course," Jack said. "You're my trail buddy."

"What about your Manhattan apartment?" Hugh asked.

"We're keeping it," Savannah said. "That way if I need to go there to see a client, we've got a place to stay."

"You can always stay in ours," Josh reminded her. "And I'm sure Treat would let you stay in his, too."

Jack said, "We appreciate that, and we might take you up on it at some point if we decide to sell."

"I can hook you up with my real estate guy to find a house here, and you can use office space in my building by the library," Treat offered.

"We were hoping you'd say that," Savannah said. "But only if you let me rent it."

Treat scoffed. "I'm not taking your money, Vanny."

"Then I'm not taking your space," she said with a defiant lift of her chin. She adored her brothers, but she liked to stand on her own two feet.

Max patted Treat's leg and said, "How about we table this discussion for later? I'm excited that you guys are going to be closer."

"We are, too. It feels right." Savannah looked at Lacy and said, "Okay, your turn. What's your news?"

"We're moving back, too!" Lacy said, and more cheers rang out.

Savannah and the girls squealed with delight. The kids popped to their feet, jumping up and down, chanting, "Finn's moving here! Finn's moving here!"

"I can't believe it!" Riley said. "I'm so excited!"

"What about your boat?" Josh asked.

Hugh shook his head. "No way you're moving to dry land."

Dane had lived on the water since graduating from college, but while Savannah's brothers might be shocked that Dane would make such a drastic lifestyle change, she wasn't. She'd seen each of her brothers change in ways she'd never imagined after they'd fallen in love with their wives. She snuggled closer to her rugged husband, knowing firsthand just what changes true love could bring.

"Whoa!" Hal said, arms outstretched. "Kids, sit on your bottoms. I want to hear Uncle Dane speak, and right now all I hear are little voices."

"My voice isn't little!" Christian exclaimed, earning laughter from everyone except Hugh.

"Don't talk back to Grandpa," Hugh scolded.

Christian scooted on his knees over to Hal and put his little hands on his grandfather's wide knees, blinking big brown eyes up at Hal. "I'm sorry, Grandpa, but I *do* have a big voice. You told me so. Remember? You said it was going to be a great man voice one day."

Hal lifted Christian onto his lap. "You're right, son. I did say that, and you do have a big voice. I guess I should have said that all I heard were *children's* voices."

"Yup," Christian agreed.

"Thanks for the lesson in semantics, son." Hal kissed Christian's head and said, "Now let's hear what Uncle Dane has to say."

"We bought a plot of land on the border of Weston and Allure, about thirty minutes from the center of town." Dane looked lovingly at Lacy and said, "We wanted to be closer to Lacy's sisters and closer to all of you. And we decided this was the perfect location to start our new business venture. We're opening an indoor/outdoor sea discovery place for kids, with a small aquarium, educational exhibits about sharks and sea creatures, and hands-on activities."

"We're hoping to host field trips and other events, like birthday parties," Lacy added. "With my marketing skills and Dane's knowledge and connections, we think it'll be a big hit."

"Noah wants to go in on it with us," Dane said. Their relative Noah Braden was a marine biologist.

"That's awesome," Treat said. "But why limit it to the sea?"

Dane shrugged. "It's what I know."

"I know the outdoors, so if you ever want to expand to include that sort of thing, I'd be interested in getting involved," Jack suggested.

"Seriously? That'd be great." Dane glanced at Lacy, who nodded excitedly.

"Hell, bro, count me in, too," Hugh said. "I've got time and money, if you want to consider teaching kids about racing, which is way cooler than sharks or mountains."

Jack scoffed. "Says who?"

Dane laughed. "Are you serious, or are you just screwing around?"

"I'm serious." Hugh's eyes lit up and he said, "Think about it. You can have a racetrack with mini cars and interactive displays where kids can shift gears and learn about driving safety while having fun." He smirked and said, "Besides, you've got the greatest racer at your fingertips. Why not use him?"

Brianna rolled her eyes and said, "My modest husband."

"When they were handing out modesty, Treat took my share," Hugh said with a playful wink at Treat.

"I think it's a great business model," Treat said. Then he chuckled and added, "*Despite* bringing racing into it."

"I think these are all fantastic ideas and would make it even more interesting for kids," Lacy said.

As Dane and Lacy told them more about their visions for the company, Hugh and Jack added their two cents.

"Sounds like the first Braden-Remington multifaceted-discovery zone is underway," Dane said. "There's just one thing I need to get approval for before we can move forward. Dad, we were hoping to stay with you while we build our house. Think that'd be okay? It might take quite a while."

The smile on Hal's face was nothing compared to the shine in his eyes. "Son, if it were up to me, I'd have every damn one of you move back in."

"We're all moving in with Grandpa!" Christian hollered as he slipped from Hal's lap.

The adults laughed, the kids cheered, and Hal said, "Looks like my Christmas wish might just come true after all."

Chapter Four

JOSH OPENED HAL'S front door, and the kids raced by and ran into the living room. "Slow down," he called after them. *I sound just like Dad used to.* He smiled to himself, thinking that wasn't such a bad thing.

"Good luck with that," Rex said, pushing past with Josslyn in his arms. "They're wired."

Josh shook his head. "I don't know how they can be after the hayride, sled riding, and lighting sparklers. I thought they'd all be worn out, like Abi." Abigail was fast asleep in Riley's arms.

"Excuse us, please," Adriana said loudly as she and Layla squeezed by with Brianna and Lacy.

"We're going to get milk and cookies for everyone," Brianna called out on her way to the kitchen.

Rex glanced in the living room, where the boys were shucking their coats, hats, and gloves. "Hey, don't leave your stuff on the floor."

"We won't!" the boys said in unison.

Rex arched a brow at Josh. "My ass they won't. Would you mind keeping an eye on Little Hal while we go change Joss?"

"She's sleeping," Josh pointed out as Jade and the others filed into the house.

"*Exactly*." Rex swatted Jade's butt, earning a giggle, and they headed up the stairs.

Treat came in carrying Bryce, who was asleep on his chest, and looked at Rex and Jade hurrying up the stairs. "Where are they going?"

"It's Rex," Josh said. "Where do you *think* they're going?"

Treat chuckled and moved aside to take off his and Bryce's coats.

"That guy has more testosterone than any ten men I know," Max said, earning an annoyed look from Treat. She quickly added, "Except you, honey. But you know that." She went up on her toes beside Treat, and Josh heard her say, "I've got a double sleeping bag for us for later."

"I did *not* need to hear that," Josh said as he took off his coat. He hung it up and went to help Riley with Abigail. As he slipped Abigail's arm out of her coat sleeve, he said, "Ri, do you think we should put her to bed upstairs?"

"And miss all the fun? No way." Riley shrugged off her coat and hung it in the closet. "This is a Braden tradition, and it means the world to your father. I want our children to love it just as much as we do."

Josh took Abigail from her and drew Riley into his arms as Max walked past with an armful of kids' coats and said, "There has to be an easier way."

"We could have a kids' house, where we let them run wild and mess things up, and then we adults can stay here," Josh suggested.

Max dropped the pile of coats by the coat closet and said, "I'm about *this close* to agreeing to that. But then the adult house would be too quiet, and we'd all end up in the kids' house anyway." She began hanging up coats, and when Riley moved to help her Max waved her away. "You two go back to what you were doing. I can handle the coats."

"Best sister-in-law ever," Josh said, and then he gathered Riley in his arms with Abigail and said, "And you're the best wife ever." He kissed her good and deep, earning a greedy moan.

"Hey, you can kiss, but I don't need sound effects," Max teased.

Riley laughed and then she gasped and said, "We almost forgot the pajamas!" She disappeared into the den and came out with the box of pajamas they'd made for all the kids and carried it into the living room. "Okay, kids, gather around! Me and Uncle Josh are introducing a new children's clothing line for the boutique we're opening at Ocean Edge, Treat's resort on Cape Cod, and we made pajamas just for you!"

"Pajamas!" Dylan hollered, and ran over with the rest of the boys on his heels like the Pied Piper.

All the boys began reaching into the box, and Treat said, "How about we let Aunt Riley hand them out?"

Dylan harrumphed. "Okay."

"Atta boy." Treat sat on the couch with Bryce, overseeing things as Riley handed out the pajamas.

"A new children's clothing line?" Jack asked. "That's exciting."

"Yes!" Riley exclaimed. "We're excited to make kids' clothes. It was Mia's idea." Mia was Josh's assistant. "We're just beginning to come up with designs, and we're starting with casual and sleepwear. We're also designing adult clothes for the boutique, of course, but we're going for a more eclectic feel."

"I'm excited to see what you come up with," Max said as she sat beside Treat.

Hugh and Dane brought in a load of sleeping bags and blankets, dumped them on the floor, took one look at the kids hopping up and down and chattering and headed toward the kitchen.

"Christian and Dylan, these are for you." Riley held up red-and-black striped bottoms and red tops with RING LEADER written across the front.

"Oh my gosh. Those are adorable!" Max exclaimed.

"Cool!" Christian hollered as he and Dylan snatched their pajamas.

"What do you say?" Max urged.

"Thank you!" they said in unison.

Riley handed pajamas to Layla and Adriana and said, "Red-and-white striped bottoms with red tops for our big girls."

"Thank you!" Adriana hugged Riley. She turned to Treat and Max, holding up her top, and said, "It has my name on it!"

Layla looked at hers and said, "Mine does, too!" She showed everyone her top with her name written in script across the chest. "I love them! Thank you!" She hugged Josh, and then she hugged Riley.

The joy in the kids' eyes made all of the long hours Josh and Riley had put into designing the pajamas in time for Christmas worth it.

"They're really gorgeous," Max said.

"Thank you." Riley beamed at Josh and said, "We're having a lot of fun with the designs."

Josh had never even considered designing clothing for children, but when Mia had brought up the idea, both he and Riley were instantly on board and wondered why they hadn't thought of it themselves. There was a lot more flexibility in designs for children than there was for adults, and if all went well the first year, they might even expand to children's formal wear.

"Come on!" Adriana took Layla's hand and said, "Let's go change in the bathroom!"

"And we've got green-and-red striped bottoms with green tops for the Three Musketeers—Finn, Adam, and Little Hal." She handed them each a pair of pajamas, and all of the boys began stripping off their clothes.

"Mini Chippendales in the living room. *Nice*," Josh said with a smile.

"And we've got adorable sleepers for Abi, Joss, and Bryce. Each one has a different design." She handed Bryce's pajamas to Max. "Where's Joss?"

"Rex and Jade took her upstairs to change her diaper and never came back down," Josh said as he reached for Riley's hand, helping her to her feet. "I think they're doing what I'd like to do."

"Ew," Savannah said as she pushed past Josh to help Adam with his pajamas. "I want to hear all about your new clothing line, *not* about what you want to do to your wife."

"Okay! I'm ready!" Little Hal shouted.

Josh glanced over and laughed. "Why are you *naked?*"

Little Hal looked down at his privates and shrugged.

"Because he's Rex's son," Hal said as he came into the room with two sleeping bags. He set them down and said, "When Rex was his age, he stripped off every stitch of clothing every chance he got. Now, come on, son, let's cover up that pickle around all these women."

"Where's Grandpa's pj's?" Little Hal asked as Grandpa knelt to help him put on his pajamas.

"Good question," Riley said as she and Josh changed Abigail into her pajamas. "We only made pj's for the kids. But I bet Grandpa has special pajamas he'll change into, too."

"Maybe Grandpa wants to be naked!" Christian said as he pulled his pajama shirt over his head.

"No!" Treat and Josh said at once.

Josh looked around and said, "Why are the rest of our brothers missing?"

"I saw Hugh and Dane go into the kitchen, probably helping with the snacks," Riley said as she picked up Abigail.

"I'll go see if I can help." He kissed Riley and then he went into the kitchen, where he found Lacy straddling Dane's lap on a chair by the window as they ate at each other's faces like libidinous beasts. Josh cleared his throat.

"Dude?" Dane glowered. "Do you mind?"

"Jesus, Dane. What if your kid came in here?" Josh grabbed a cookie.

Lacy giggled and said, "He's caught us kissing before. Hasn't Abi ever toddled in and caught you and Riley in a compromising position?"

Josh grinned. "Okay, moving on...Have you seen Hugh?"

Dane pointed to the pantry and smirked. "Bree went in with him."

"All right, you know what? The hell with this. My wife and I need some make-out time, too. How about y'all watch our baby for a while?"

Lacy gave Dane a quick kiss and slithered off his lap, "I will!" She hurried past Josh, patting him on the shoulder on the way out.

"You suck," Dane said to Josh.

"Finn's three and he's got the other boys to keep him busy. Abi needs us twenty-four-seven, so yeah, I'm gonna suck for twenty minutes in your eyes, but in my wife's eyes?" Josh snickered. "I'll be a sex god."

Riley came into the kitchen as he said *sex god* and as she pressed her body to his, she said, "Baby, you surpassed sex-god status when we christened our dining room table. Come on, Lacy said we have half an hour."

As they left the room, Dane called after them, "I'm never eating at your house again!"

DANE HEADED INTO the living room to check on his boy and see if he could convince his gorgeous wife to sneak away with him again. *Damn cock-blocking Josh.* But the truth was, Dane couldn't blame him. At three, Finn could entertain himself for a little while, but he remembered all too clearly what it had been like when Finn was younger. He chuckled to himself, recalling the hurry-up sex they'd had in the kitchen while Finn was watching television and on the deck of the boat while he was sleeping down below. Kids were the best and worst form of birth control, because they made it so hard to find time to have sex, and when they did, birth control was the last thing on Dane's mind. Unfortunately, he and Lacy had not been blessed with another child, which was another reason they were settling down on dry land. Though they'd decided not to mention it to their family until they'd been approved, they hoped to adopt after they were in their new home.

The living room was controlled chaos. Everyone was busy setting up sleeping bags, arranging pillows, and spreading out blankets for their slumber party. And there in the center of it all was Lacy reading to Finn. Finn sat on her lap, clinging to his blue stuffed shark, Chomper. Lacy had a way of tuning everything out except their son, and that was only one of the things he loved about her. She'd always been the calm to Dane's storm, the anchor that kept him grounded.

She looked up, catching him staring. She smiled, and it reached all the way up to her pretty blue eyes. He felt her love right in the center of his chest, burrowing into his heart. He never thought he could love anyone as much as he loved her and Finn, but every day that love grew to new proportions.

His father sidled up to him and draped a heavy arm around his shoulder. "You have a beautiful family, son."

"Thanks, Dad."

"Your mother is smiling down on us, pleased as punch that y'all are still carrying on her slumber party tradition."

"I know, Dad." Dane knew his father believed he had full-on conversations with their late mother, and for a long time Dane had pitied him. But then Dane had met Lacy, and it was Lacy's voice he heard whispering in his ear when he was deep-sea diving, tagging sharks, and doing under-water research. Those whispers made a believer out of him, because he knew without a shadow of a doubt that their love was strong enough to transcend anything—and from what he'd seen and heard, his parents' love was just as real.

"Look at your boy with Lacy, calm as ever in the middle of all this noise," Hal said. "You and your mama were the same way."

"Yeah?" He liked knowing that.

"Yes, sir. Like two peas in a pod, you two were. A little bird told me there's another reason you're moving back. Anything you want to share with me?"

Dane looked curiously at him. "How is it that you always know when I'm keeping something from everyone?"

Hal grinned and said, "What I don't know from father-ly intuition, a certain bird whispers in my ear."

"Mom, *right*. Well, Pop, we're thinking of adopting once we're settled. Luke gave us the name of the agency he and Daisy used, and we're starting the process after the New Year." Luke and his wife, Daisy, had recently adopted a sweet one-year-old girl from Guyana named Kendal.

"That's absolutely wonderful, but why wouldn't you want to share that with the others?"

"Because I don't need to be given shit about my *slow swimmers*," he said honestly.

"I think you underestimate your siblings," Hal said seriously. "They're full of gumption, but they're not animals."

Dane scoffed. "I've done enough bragging about my anatomical *gift*. I'm due whatever shit they give me, but I don't want to hear it over Christmas."

Hal chuckled. "I won't argue with that. But I love knowing you and your little lady are going to give a heck of a good life to a child who needs it. I'm proud of you, son. Now, do me a favor and go drag your brother and Jade out of their love nest so we can get this movie night started."

Chapter Five

THE CHILDREN CRAWLED all over the blankets and sleeping bags, playing with toys and anxiously awaiting cookies, chocolate milk, and the movie. The annual slumber party was one of Rex's favorite family gatherings. The noise and craziness reminded him of when their mother was still alive. He was only eight when she died, but he'd never forget the way her positive energy used to light up a room. She would rearrange the furniture for the slumber party, and then rearrange it again in the middle of the festivities because something *just didn't feel right.* She was all about energy flow and positivity, and she had the innate ability to quiet her rascally children with a single look, just like Hal could. Rex didn't know how his parents had kept up with the six of them, but as his gaze drifted to his father sitting beside Treat on the couch, the gratitude and respect he felt for the man who had kept their family together at a time when he'd probably wanted to fall apart made his chest ache.

"Who ate all of the Christmas tree cookies?" Max asked as she came out of the kitchen with a trayful of crumbs, staring at Hugh and Dane.

"Hey, don't look at me," Hugh said.

Max sighed. "You and Dane were the last ones in the kitchen."

Rex's eyes went straight to Little Hal, who was known for sneaking cookies, but Hal was looking around the room for the culprit, too. Rex heard a giggle come from behind the couch and stepped around it. He found Dylan and Christian shoving cookies into their mouths as fast as their hands would allow. Their pajamas were covered in crumbs.

They tipped their faces up, wide-eyed, mouths full of cookies, and red and green sugar on their lips, and said, "We didn't do it."

Laughter bubbled out before Rex could stop it. He took their arms and lifted them to their feet. "I think I found the culprits." He gave them each a pat on their butts, nudging them toward their parents, and said, "Make 'em wash dishes for a week."

"I've got better plans for them," Max said. "Dylan Braden, get over here."

"Why am I not surprised our son is involved?" Brianna

eyed Hugh, who reached for Christian's hand.

Josh laughed and said, "Because he's *Hugh's* son."

Hugh glowered at him.

"I *am* yours, Daddy," Christian said, spitting crumbs everywhere.

"You might not want to say that so proudly, little dude," Dane said with a chuckle.

"You're lucky we made several dozen other cookies," Max said as she knelt beside Dylan. "You owe your cousins an apology for eating all those cookies, and tomorrow morning you are going to help with breakfast to make up for it."

"Sorry for eating the cookies!" Dylan exclaimed, and then with a big grin he said, "Can me and Christian make rocket pancakes for breakfast? Remember when Charlotte made them?"

Max turned beet red, and all the adults tried—and failed—to hold in their laughter. Josh and Riley had gotten married at the Sterling House, the same location where Hal and their mother had gotten married. Though at the time the rustic inn had no longer functioned as a resort, the owner, Charlotte Sterling, an erotic romance writer, lived there. She was now engaged to their relative Beau Braden, and they were renovating the inn. But when Rex and his family had arrived for the weekend of the wedding,

Charlotte was making pancakes in the shape of penises, acting out a scene she was crafting for one of her books. Thinking quickly, she'd told the kids they were rocket ships. From what Rex had heard, Charlotte still acted out the scenes she crafted, and things got a lot spicier than pancakes.

Max cleared her throat, glancing furtively at Treat, who pushed to his feet and said, "Come on, Dylan. Let's go have a talk."

"About rocket pancakes?" Dylan asked.

"About sharing and not being selfish," Treat said as they left the room.

Hugh and Christian followed them out, passing Lacy and Riley, who were on their way into the living room with trays of sippy cups.

"The other cookies are ready to come out," Lacy said as she set down the tray.

"I'll get them," Jade said, giving Rex a *follow-me* look as she headed into the kitchen.

His insides thrummed with desire. He knew his brothers thought they'd been going at it upstairs earlier, but they had it all wrong. Jade had just given birth to their beautiful baby girl a few weeks ago. She was tired, and her body wasn't ready for their animalistic lovemaking. But they'd enjoyed every private second of lying in each other's arms naked, kissing and snuggling without worrying about Little Hal barging in.

Rex headed for the kitchen, but Dane grabbed his arm, stopping him. Rex arched a brow and said, "Got a problem, bro?"

Amusement rose in Dane's eyes. "If you go into that kitchen, you'll end up in the bedroom with your wife again, and then we'll have to wait to start the movie. And *that's* not going to happen."

Rex chuckled. "Whose turn is it to pick the movie this year, anyway?"

"Mine," Josh said from his perch on one of the recliners, where he was holding Abigail. "I choose *Miracle on 34th Street*. It's a classic."

"Actually, I think it's mine," Rex said. "We're watching *A Christmas Story*."

"I don't think our kids need to hear about shooting their eyes out," Dane said.

"Who shot their eyes out?" Adriana asked, starting a litany of questions.

As the adults fielded questions and told the kids about *A Christmas Story*, Jade and Lacy returned with trays of cookies and set them on the coffee table. The kids jumped up and down, gathering around to choose their treats.

"One for each hand, not *five*," Lacy reminded them.

"But Dylan and Christian ate a whole tray!" Little Hal hollered.

"And they're lucky we didn't string them up by their feet," Treat said as he and Dylan came into the living room.

Jade walked seductively to Rex and wrapped her arms around him. She pushed her hands into his back pockets, looking curiously up at him, and said, "You left me hanging for the first time in our adult lives. Should I be worried?"

"No, babe. Dane snagged me, and I'll make it up to you for the rest of my life." He pressed his lips to hers, then whispered in her ear all the dirty things he'd like to do to her when she was ready.

"Oh *my*." She fanned her face as his siblings argued over who was going to choose the movie.

"Um, no, sorry," Savannah chimed in from her seat between Adam and Jack on a sleeping bag by the Christmas tree. "It's *my* pick this year, and we're watching *It's a Wonderful Life*."

"No way," Dane said. "It's *my* turn, and we're spending Christmas with the Griswolds."

Savannah groaned.

"That's right. *National Lampoon's Christmas Vacation*, the best Christmas movie *ever*." Dane flashed a cheesy smile at Savannah.

"How about Rudolph?" Brianna asked, rubbing her protruding belly.

Riley grabbed a cookie and said, "I can't believe nobody has suggested *Elf*. There is no better Christmas movie."

"No way. *The Grinch* rules." Hugh piped in with, "Who votes for *How the Grinch Stole Christmas*?"

The kids began chanting, "Grinch! Grinch! Grinch!"

Rex sat on the couch, pulled Jade down onto his lap, and said, "I don't care what we watch as long as we don't have to move."

Treat stepped into the middle of the room with the air of authority he had long ago earned, which went beyond just being the eldest. It was Treat who made sure that each one of them remembered their mother. Savannah, Josh, and Hugh had been so young when she died, they had no real memories of her, but Treat filled them in every chance he got, telling endless stories that even Rex hadn't remembered.

"This is my year," Treat announced. "I brought the perfect movie, and I know we'll all enjoy it. Why don't the kids settle into their sleeping bags and blankets, and then we'll get started."

ONCE EVERYONE WAS settled, Treat dimmed the lights and took a seat beside his father, who was sitting in his leather recliner. Treat knew that particular chair had been their mother's favorite before it had been their father's. He put his hand on Hal's forearm and said, "This is for you, Dad. Merry Christmas."

The television screen above the fireplace came to life, and a panoramic video Treat had taken of his father's property appeared. It began with the house where Hal and Adriana had started their lives together, the house where Treat and his siblings had been raised, and then the camera panned slowly to the woods beyond, which now led to Treat and Max's house. It continued to the horse pastures where their mother used to ride, the mountains looming in the distance, where their family had spent countless hours hiking and horseback riding. And finally, the barns appeared and BECOMING BRADENS flashed on the screen.

"What *is* this?" Savannah asked with awe, and everyone shushed her.

Hal eyed Treat. "You made this?"

Treat nodded. He'd spent the last year going through their family photos to create this keepsake for his father, and for generations to come. He turned his eyes back to the movie so his father wouldn't miss a second of it. A black-and-white picture of his parents taken the year they'd met, when his mother had been only fourteen, appeared on the screen. They were standing by the fence where they'd met on her father's property. She was tall and slim with long hair and a smile that radiated off the screen. It was like looking at Savannah as a teenager. Their father had a mop of dark hair, and though he was only a teenager, he was already big and broad.

"Oh my God," Savannah said. "Tissues, Jack. *Quick.*"

Jack got up, and Riley said, "For me, too, please."

The other women asked for some, too, as the next picture of his parents appeared, both on horseback, leaning across the space between them, kissing.

"Is that Grandma?" Layla asked.

"It is, honey," Hugh said, pulling her closer.

"She's beautiful," Layla said. "She looks just like you, Adriana. No wonder they named you after her."

"Adriana looks like her," Brianna corrected her. "And they're both beautiful, just like you are."

Adriana left her sleeping bag and went to Hal. "Can I sit on your lap, Grandpa?"

Hal patted his thigh, and she climbed up. He kissed her head and said, "Love you, darlin'."

Treat heard the emotions Hal was holding back, and

his own throat thickened. He'd always wished his siblings could have had more time to get to know their mother the way he had. He'd been nine when she fell ill and eleven when she'd died. And not a day passed that he didn't find himself sending thoughts about his family up to her.

"I love you, too, Grandpa," Adriana said as another picture of her late grandmother flashed on the screen. She was standing beneath a big tree, and Hal was down on one knee in front of her, presenting her with a bouquet of wildflowers.

"Oh, Daddy," Savannah said tearfully. "You're such a romantic."

"And handsome," Max said.

Hal didn't say a word. His damp eyes were trained on the television as more pictures rolled through. There was a picture of Treat's first Christmas, his mother smiling down at him in her arms, his father gazing at her, and a picture of Treat, Dane, and Rex as young boys sitting on the fence by the barn. There was one of Adriana holding baby Josh, with Savannah sitting beside her, while Treat, Rex, and Dane played with trucks nearby. The next was of Adriana lying on a blanket on the beach in front of the house on Cape Cod where they used to vacation, which Treat now owned. Treat and Rex were playing by the water in the distance. There were pictures of his father, broad and muscled, working with the horses and manning the barbecue with the kids nearby, and a photograph of Adriana sitting on Hope with her arms around Savannah, who couldn't have been more than two years old.

"That's Hope!" Dylan said.

"That means that was after she got sick," Josh said softly.

"Right after," Treat confirmed. Treat would never forget the heartbreak of watching his mother wither away right before their eyes—or his desperation to keep her alive.

More pictures appeared, photographs Treat remembered taking of his parents holding hands, kissing, and walking by the barn. He'd taken them with the camera his parents had bought him for his eighth birthday. He'd taken most of those pictures without their knowledge, though they'd found out as soon as they'd had the film developed.

The adults sniffled, making appreciative sounds, as the children called out comments like, "Look, there's my dad!" "Is that Uncle Rex or Grandpa?" and "Look at those kids! They're covered in mud!"

Treat, Rex, and Dane were in fact covered from head to toe in that picture. They'd gone down to a creek, even though their father had told them not to because it had been raining for days. They'd been covered in mud from the trek through the woods, and then Dane had gone into the water to clean off. Treat had gone after him, and then they'd all ended up in the water, laughing and wrestling. The walk home had also included a few muddy grappling matches. They'd all been grounded and given extra chores for what had felt like months after that little excursion, but it'd been worth it. Their mother had taken a turn for the worse by then, and they'd needed to work through their emotions.

The movie included small clips Treat had rescued from old reels his parents had taken, of birthday parties and holidays. Hearing his mother's voice broke the dam on his sadness, even though he'd seen the movie a dozen or more times. But he wasn't ashamed, and he let his tears fall, as did his siblings.

Hal reached over and squeezed Treat's hand, tears sliding down his rugged, sun-kissed cheeks, a world of gratitude showing in his eyes, and then he returned his attention to the television, as their lives played out before them.

There was a clip of Adriana's last Christmas. She had lost a lot of weight, and she was sitting in the recliner where Hal currently sat, bundled up in the quilt Hal still slept with. She was holding baby Hugh on her lap. Rex and Dane were shaking presents near the tree, and Savannah sat with a stuffed teddy bear in her lap. Treat stood beside his mother's chair and said, "Put the presents down."

Young Rex frowned and snapped, "You're not the boss of me!" in a voice that sounded too deep for an eight-year-old boy.

Their mother laughed, as did everyone who was watching the movie. Treat remembered that day like it was yesterday, and he'd give anything to have it back.

The next image that appeared was of his mother lying in her bed a few days before she passed away, with her children beside her. She was smiling, and though she was gaunt, her skin ashen, and her body too frail to move, in her eyes was love as real as the world they lived in. There was no holding back tears for any of them.

Savannah buried her face in Jack's chest, and Adam asked, "Why you crying, Mama?"

"I'm just happy to see my mom," she said. "I feel her all around me."

"Me too," Rex said as the next picture appeared, of Hugh on his fifth birthday.

They were all gathered around the picnic table in the yard. Hugh was leaning over the cake, his cheeks puffed up to blow out the candles. Rex wore a cowboy hat, his thick black hair brushing his collar the same way he wore it today. Hugh, Savannah, and Josh wore pointy paper birthday hats. Treat stood beside Hope, who was also wearing a pointy paper hat because Hugh had insisted.

Little Hal jumped up and down and said, "Look at Hope's hat!"

"That's silly!" Finn said.

"I want Hope to wear a hat on my birthday!" Adam exclaimed.

"Is that Christian? Why wasn't I at his party?" Dylan asked.

"No, buddy," Treat said. "That's his daddy's fifth birthday party."

More pictures appeared, of Rex as a burly teen training a horse, Hal dancing with seven-year-old Savannah at the Christmas barn dance, Josh's high school graduation, and Dane with his first boat. The more pictures that appeared, the bigger Hal's smile grew. He watched Savannah's college graduation, Treat standing before the first resort he'd ever purchased, and more recent pictures, of weddings and grandbabies.

The second to last picture appeared, of Hal sitting in his recliner last Christmas, surrounded by all his grandchildren, and the girls *aww*ed.

When the final picture appeared, of Hal and Adriana

kissing on their wedding day, Hal's cowboy hat tipping off his head, both of them smiling so brightly, Treat swore he felt a gust of warm wind move through the room.

Dane looked over, brows knitted. "Did you feel that?"

"Yeah," Josh and Hugh said in unison.

"She's with us, boys. She's always with us," Hal said as a *thud* sounded on the patio door, startling the girls.

They all looked over and saw Hope watching them through the glass.

"Oh no! Someone left Hope's stall open," Adriana said.

Treat and Hal exchanged a tearful smile.

"No, darlin'," Hal said. "Hope just has a way of knowing when we need her most."

Want More Bradens?

I hope you loved spending Christmas Eve with the Bradens. If this is your first Braden book, you might want to read each of the Bradens at Weston love stories, starting with the full-length novel LOVERS AT HEART, REIMAGINED, Treat and Max's love story. All of my books may be enjoyed as stand-alone romances. Jump in at any time!

New to the Love in Bloom series?

The Love in Bloom big-family romance collection features several families. Characters from each series appear in future Love in Bloom books. Find free downloadable series reading order and publication order checklists, family trees, and more on Melissa's Reader Goodies page: www.MelissaFoster.com/RG.

Please enjoy this preview of
LOVERS AT HEART, REIMAGINED

Chapter One

TREAT BRADEN DIDN'T usually charter planes. It wasn't his style to flash his wealth. But today he needed to be anywhere but his Nassau resort, and missing his commercial flight had just plain pissed him off. He owned upscale resorts all over the world, and he'd been featured on travel shows so many times that it turned his stomach to have to play those ridiculous media games. Most of the pomp and circumstance surrounding him had begun to irk him in ways that it never had before meeting Max Armstrong. It had been too many long, lonely weeks since he'd seen her standing in the lobby of his Nassau resort, since his heart first thundered in a way that threw him completely off-kilter—and since they'd spent one incredible evening together. Treat wasn't a Neanderthal. He'd known he had no claim on her, even after their intimate evening. Hell, they hadn't even slept together. But that hadn't stopped his blood from boiling or kept him from acting like a jerk the next morning when he'd seen her with another man in front of the elevators, wearing the same clothes she'd had on when Treat had left her the night before.

He hadn't been able to stop thinking about Max since the moment he'd first met her, despite the uncomfortable encounter, but he'd been burned before, and he wasn't into repeating his mistakes. Getting away from resorts altogether and spending a weekend with his father at his ranch in Weston, Colorado, a small ranch town with dusty streets, too many cowboy hats, and a main drag that had been built to replicate the Wild West, was just what he needed.

His rental SUV moved at a snail's pace behind a line of traffic that was not at all typical for his hometown. It wasn't until he crawled around the next curve and saw balloons and banners above the road announcing the annual Indie Film Festival that he realized what weekend it was. He wasn't in the mood to deal with crowds.

His cell phone rang, and his sister's name flashed on the screen. *Savannah.* Before he could say hello, she said, "I can't believe you didn't call me before you came out."

"Hi, sis. I miss you, too." The only girl among his five siblings, Savannah was a cutthroat entertainment attorney, but to Treat she'd always be his baby sister.

"You big oaf," she said with a laugh. "I'm at the festival with a client. When will you get in?"

"I'm here now, sitting in traffic on Main Street." He hadn't moved an inch in five minutes.

"Yeah? Come to the festival and see me. I'll wait for you at the rear entrance."

All he really wanted to do was reach his father's two-hundred-acre ranch just outside of town, but Treat knew that if he didn't see Savannah right away, she'd be disappointed. Disappointing his siblings was something he strived not to do. Having lost their mother when Treat was only eleven and his youngest sibling, Hugh, had been hardly more than a baby, his siblings had already faced enough disappointment for one lifetime.

"You're with a client. Sure you can get away?" he asked.

"Who are you kidding? For you? Of course. Besides, I'm with Connor Dean. He can handle things for a little while. Come in the back gate. I'll wait there." Connor was an actor who was quickly climbing the ranks of fame. Savannah had been his attorney for two years, and whenever he had a public engagement, he brought her along. It wasn't a typical attorney-client relationship, but for all of

Connor's bravado, he'd been slandered one too many times. Savannah kept track of what was and wasn't said at most events—by both Connor and the media.

"I'll be there as soon as traffic allows." After he ended the call with Savannah he called his father.

"Hey there, son."

Hal's slow, deep drawl tugged at Treat's heart. He'd missed him. Hal had always been a calming influence on Treat. After his mother passed away, his father had pulled him and his siblings through those tumultuous years. But Hal wasn't a coddler. He had instilled a strong work ethic and sense of loyalty into their heads, and that had enabled each of them to be successful in their endeavors.

"Dad, I'm here in town, but I'm going to stop at the festival first to see Savannah, if you don't mind."

"Yup. Savannah called. Treat, enjoy your time with her. She misses you, and I'd venture a guess that you could use a little extended family time, too."

He could say that again. Anything to keep his mind off Max.

To continue reading, please buy
LOVERS AT HEART, REIMAGINED

More Books By Melissa Foster

Love in Bloom Romance Collection

Love in Bloom books may be read as stand alones. For more enjoyment, read them in series order. Characters from each series carry forward to the next.

SNOW SISTERS

Sisters in Love
Sisters in Bloom
Sisters in White

THE BRADENS (Weston, CO)

Lovers at Heart, Reimagined
Destined for Love
Friendship on Fire
Sea of Love
Bursting with Love
Hearts at Play

THE BRADENS (Trusty, CO)

Taken by Love
Fated for Love
Romancing My Love
Flirting with Love
Dreaming of Love
Crashing into Love

THE BRADENS (Peaceful Harbor, MD)

Healed by Love
Surrender My Love

River of Love
Crushing on Love
Whisper of Love
Thrill of Love

THE BRADENS & MONTGOMERYS (Pleasant Hill – Oak Falls)
Embracing Her Heart
Anything for Love
Trails of Love
Wild, Crazy Hearts
Making You Mine

BRADEN WORLD NOVELLAS
Daring Her Love
Promise My Love
Our New Love
Story of Love
Love at Last

THE REMINGTONS
Game of Love
Stroke of Love
Flames of Love
Slope of Love
Read, Write, Love
Touched by Love

SEASIDE SUMMERS
Seaside Dreams
Seaside Hearts
Seaside Sunsets
Seaside Secrets

Seaside Nights

Seaside Embrace

Seaside Lovers

Seaside Whispers

BAYSIDE SUMMERS

Bayside Desires

Bayside Passions

Bayside Heat

Bayside Escape

Bayside Romance

THE RYDERS

Seized by Love

Claimed by Love

Chased by Love

Rescued by Love

Swept Into Love

SUGAR LAKE

The Real Thing

Only for You

Love Like Ours

Finding My Girl

TRU BLUE & THE WHISKEYS

Tru Blue (Set in Peaceful Harbor)

Truly, Madly, Whiskey

Driving Whiskey Wild

Wicked Whiskey Love

Mad About Moon

Taming My Whiskey

WILD BOYS (Billionaires After Dark)

Logan

Heath

Jackson

Cooper

BAD BOYS (Billionaires After Dark)

Mick

Dylan

Carson

Brett

HARBORSIDE NIGHTS

Includes characters from the Love in Bloom series

Catching Cassidy

Discovering Delilah

Tempting Tristan

Standalone Books by Melissa

Chasing Amanda (mystery/suspense)

Come Back to Me (mystery/suspense)

Have No Shame (historical fiction/romance)

Love, Lies & Mystery (3-book bundle)

Megan's Way (literary fiction)

Traces of Kara (psychological thriller)

Where Petals Fall (suspense)

Meet Melissa

www.MelissaFoster.com

Melissa Foster is a *New York Times* and *USA Today* bestselling and award-winning author. Her books have been recommended by *USA Today's* book blog, *Hagerstown* magazine, *The Patriot*, and several other print venues. Melissa has painted and donated several murals to the Hospital for Sick Children in Washington, DC.

Visit Melissa on her website or chat with her on social media. Melissa enjoys discussing her books with book clubs and reader groups and welcomes an invitation to your event. Melissa's books are available through most online retailers in paperback, digital, and audio formats.

9 781948 868334